Text copyright © 2006 by Harriet Ziefert, Inc.
Illustrations copyright © 2006 by Teetersaw, Inc.
All rights reserved
CIP Data is available.
Published in the United States 2006 by
🍎 Blue Apple Books
P.O. Box 1380, Maplewood, N.J. 07040
www.blueapplebooks.com
Distributed in the U.S. by Chronicle Books
First Edition
Printed in China

ISBN 13: 978-1-59354-170-5
ISBN 10: 1-59354-170-8

1   3   5   7   9   10   8   6   4   2

I CAN WAIT
for the Bell to Ring!

DRAWINGS BY JENNIFER RAPP

BLUE APPLE BOOKS

Some days are terrific.
Everything clicks.
You don't wait for anything.
Everything moves quick!

The bus arrives.
You're on time for school.
You say to yourself,
"Today will be cool!"

THEN...
You wait in line.
You wait for your turn.
You wait for the bell.
Your mind starts to churn!

SO...
You say to yourself,
"I can be patient.
I will be patient.
I MUST BE patient.
I CAN WAIT!"

I CAN WAIT . . .

for my braces
to come off.

I CAN WAIT . . .

for a cell phone.

I CAN WAIT . . .

for the gym teacher
to stop explaining.

I CAN WAIT . . .

for my jeans
to dry.

I CAN WAIT...

for the download
to finish.

I CAN WAIT . . .

for the dog
to poop.

I CAN WAIT...

for my allowance.

I CAN WAIT...

for a snow day.

I CAN WAIT . . .

for the scab
to fall off.

I CAN WAIT...

for my dad
to see my
report card.

for my little brother
to fall asleep.

I CAN WAIT...

for the boys in my class
to get taller.

I CAN WAIT . . .

for the cheese
to cool off.

I CAN WAIT . . .

to get a haircut.

I CAN WAIT . . .   for my parents to go out.

I CAN WAIT...

for the nurse
to put alcohol
on my cut.

BUT...

I CAN'T
WAIT ...

for the
last day
of school!

Kim gave Joseph half of the pencils she received from Douglas.
Joseph kept 8 of those pencils and gave the remaining 10 to Darlene.

How many pencils did Douglas give Kim?

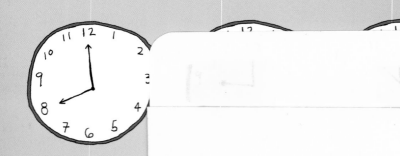

WARD COUNTY PUBLIC LIBRARY

MINOT, NORTH DAKOTA

FOR RENEWAL, CALL: 852-5388

OR TOLL FREE: 1-800-932-8932

KENMARE BRANCH: 385-4090

DEMCO